Game Over!

Dealing with Bullies

by Anastasia Suen
illustrated by Jeff Ebbeler

Content Consultant:
Vicki F. Panaccione, PhD
Licensed Child Psychologist
Founder, Better Parenting Institute

Brittan Acres School

visit us at
www.abdopublishing.com

Published by Magic Wagon, a division of the ABDO Publishing Group, 8000 West 78th Street, Edina, Minnesota, 55439. Copyright © 2009 by Abdo Consulting Group, Inc. International copyrights reserved in all countries. All rights reserved. No part of this book may be reproduced in any form without written permission from the publisher.

Looking Glass Library™ is a trademark and logo of Magic Wagon.

Printed in the United States.

Text by Anastasia Suen
Illustrations by Jeff Ebbeler
Edited by Patricia Stockland
Interior layout and design by Becky Daum
Cover design by Nicole Brecke

Library of Congress Cataloging-in-Publication Data

Suen, Anastasia.
  Game over : dealing with bullies / by Anastasia Suen ; illustrated by Jeff Ebbeler.
      p. cm. — (Main Street School. Kids with character)
   ISBN 978-1-60270-270-7
  [1. Bullies—Fiction.] I. Ebbeler, Jeffrey, ill. II. Title.
  PZ7.S94343Gam 2008
  [E]—dc22
                                        2008002861

Click! Click! Click! Dalton pressed the buttons on his handheld game. "I'm done with this level."

"Already?" asked Isaiah. "You just started at the beginning of recess."

3

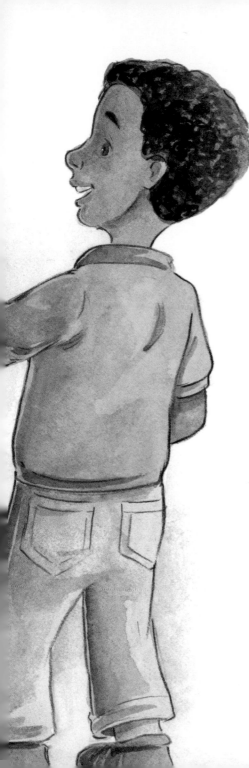

"That's impossible," said Alex.

"For you, maybe," said
Isaiah, "but not for Dalton."

"Let me see that," said Alex.

"Be my guest," said Dalton.
He handed the game to Alex.

Tyler glared across the playground at the boys.

"What kind of game is that?" he sneered. "A game for sissies?"

None of the boys said anything to Tyler.

"I still can't believe you beat that level so fast," said Alex to Dalton.

"I've been practicing," said Dalton.

"He played nonstop on the bus this morning," said Isaiah.

"I played my game on the bus, too," said Alex. "But I'm nowhere near that level."

"Me neither," said Isaiah.

"Look at these patterns!" said Alex. "This is a really hard level."

Dalton looked over at Isaiah and Alex.
Tyler was still there, watching them. *What is he doing?* wondered Dalton.

"I said, 'Is that a game for sissies?'"
repeated Tyler, walking toward them.

Alex and Isaiah just looked at the game.
Neither of them looked up at Tyler.

"Let me see that," Isaiah said to Alex.

Suddenly, Tyler swatted the game out of Isaiah's hands. "Can't you hear me?" he shouted.

Ring!

Recess was over. Tyler spun around to go inside.

"What should we do?" asked Isaiah. He reached down and picked up Dalton's game.

"Sorry about your game," said Alex. "I guess we should have said something to Tyler. But we're just supposed to ignore people like that, right?"

"That's okay," said Dalton, putting his game away. "He's just a bully. He'll probably leave us alone now. Let's just get back to class."

After school, the boys waited in line for their bus.

"Do you think you can reach the next level before you get home?" Alex asked Dalton.

"I don't know," said Dalton. "I've been working on that one for a while."

"Oh no," said Isaiah. "Here comes Tyler."

Tyler got in line behind Dalton. "How's your game going, sissy?" he asked.

Dalton didn't answer. Suddenly, Tyler grabbed the handheld from Dalton.

"Now what are you going to do?"
Tyler asked.

The boys looked at each other. They wanted to get the game back, but they were afraid of Tyler. Besides, what could they do to a big fifth grader?

19

Tyler was still laughing as he got on the bus. He laughed all the way to his seat, waving Dalton's game in the air.

Dalton had enough. "Miss Cooper," he said to the bus driver, "Tyler just took my game. I don't want to tattle, but I need it back."

Miss Cooper looked back in the mirror at Tyler. He was still laughing.

"I'll tell you what," Miss Cooper said to Dalton, "just take your seat, and I'll take care of Tyler."

Isaiah, Alex, and Dalton sat down. "I wonder what she's going to do," Alex whispered to Isaiah.

"I don't know," Isaiah answered. "But Tyler better watch out."

"I just hope I get my game back in one piece," muttered Dalton.

Soon, Miss Cooper was walking Tyler down the bus aisle. "Tyler, I believe you have something to say to Dalton," she said.

"Here's your game back," Tyler said quietly.

"And?" asked Miss Cooper.

"And I shouldn't have taken it from you," Tyler answered.

Dalton smiled a little. "Thanks for giving my game back, Tyler."

With that, Tyler got off the bus. He had to go speak with his teacher about bullying.

"Wow," said Isaiah to Dalton. "That was really brave of you to say something to Miss Cooper!"

"Yeah!" said Alex. "And it was brave of you to say something back to Tyler."

"Well, I guess he won't be bothering us anymore," said Dalton. "Back to my game!"

What Do You Think?

1. What do you think about how Tyler acted toward the boys?

2. Why did Dalton, Alex, and Isaiah ignore Tyler?

3. Why did Dalton talk to Miss Cooper?

4. Do you think Dalton did the right thing?

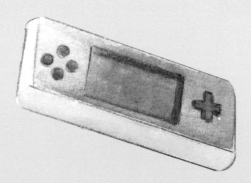

Words to Know

handheld—a small game-playing unit.
ignore—to not pay attention to something or someone.
mutter—to speak in a low voice so others can't hear you.
sneer—to speak or write in a way that puts down or makes fun of someone.

Miss K's Classroom Rules

1. Be courageous, stand up for yourself.
2. Protect your friends.
3. Tell the truth.
4. Be kind.

Web Sites

To learn more about dealing with bullies, visit ABDO Publishing Company on the World Wide Web at **www.abdopublishing.com**. Web sites about bullies are featured on our Book Links page. These links are routinely monitored and updated to provide the most current information available.